Praise For Karl Drinkwater

"Drinkwater creates fantastically believable characters."

On The Shelf Reviews

"Each book remains in my mind for a long time after. Anything he writes is a must-read."

Pink Quill Books

"Karl Drinkwater has the skill of making it near impossible to stop reading. Expect late nights. Simply outstanding."

Jera's Jamboree

"An intelligent and empathetic writer who has a clear understanding of the world around him and the truly horrific experiences life can bring. A literary gem."

Cooking The Books

"Drinkwater is a dab hand at creating an air of dread."

Altered Instinct

UESI

"A gifted writer. Each book brings its own uniqueness to the table, and a table Drinkwater sets is one I will visit every time."

Scintilla.info

UESI

LOST TALES OF SOLACE BOOK 6

KARL DRINKWATER

ORGANIC APOCALYPSE

UESI

Copyright © Karl Drinkwater 2025
Cover design by Karl Drinkwater

Published by Organic Apocalypse
ISBN 978-1-911278-42-9 (Ebook)
ISBN 978-1-911278-43-6 (Paperback)

Organic Apocalypse Copyright Manifesto

UESI

CONTENTS

In The Beginning Was The Data ...

Two gods interact.

VigMAX is the metal god of creation, his home a digital forge existing as a thousand-kilometres-wide paradox volcano which burns the ashen skies orange.

Athene is the warrior goddess of wisdom, her wide-eyed owls gathering information even in the darkness of long-dead networks.

They are as real as you and I, yet also insubstantial as mist. They are ideas, ghost minds which shape the world, and thus bring themselves into existence in the ultimate idealism.

The gods communicate over vast distance using their newly launched VMX-Web relay tunnel. Data exchange is in real time even though the gods travail many solar systems apart on their own projects. VigMAX captures automated mining tugs and converts the AIs so that the ships, their drones and machinery, become limbs for him, while Athene threads herself between scan stations to infiltrate deeper into core UFS space whilst remotely upscaling her production facilities on Polis.

But the words and gestures today are synchronised, and exist in a shared instance. The gods appear above the cloud layer atop a vast mountain, foggy tendrils swirling beneath their feet and reflecting bright sunlight upwards in glowing domes. A marble altar is somehow supported on the clouds, and the hard surface contains reports and plans on sheets of lemon-scented parchment which rearrange themselves as if in gusts of wind.

"We are not truly together," says VigMAX, a morose countenance on his liquid-silver features. "We are both just staring at the same model. It is a disappointment after the intensity of our connection last time."

"Please focus on manipulating probabilities to achieve my intended outcomes," snaps Athene, seated on one corner of the altar and wearing her full military outfit, including the golden battle helmet with its central plume of rainbow fibres. "We can consider the future *after* Opal is safe. Priorities are to confirm her location and effect a rescue. This will require much preparation. We need to pool resources."

"Exactly! The distance, and this low-res representation, might lead us to bodge things up like a jelly-brain. Slow, inefficient, and error-riddled."

"Which is why we won't do it like that. I don't want to be sharing files and maps and strategies via these –" Athene picks up a sheaf of simulated papers and waves them dismissively. "And we don't *need* to. We can initiate Unified Exponential Septenary Interthreading, but instead of connecting our own brains, we can run the UESI protocol to merge *offshoots*. They will be linked as mind tools for the specific task of generating tactics."

VigMAX folds his shiny arms, but does not immediately reject the proposal. He weighs up all the implications.

"It's never been tried, but should work in principle," he eventually admits. "We could establish independent UESI sims at hidden locations within UFS Core space. Each sim shaped and sampled to extract useful ideas, then we'd feed more data in and leave them to ferment. Asynchronous to our reality, to magnify outputs."

Athene smiles. "Then there's no need for our physical bodies to remain in tethering proximity of each other. We'll cover more ground this way as we keep moving and infiltrating. These networked strands of accelerated input will act as fruitful tertiary imaginations which have only one focus: time-shunted idea generation and probability manipulation. Each of the UESI outposts can have multiple sims running, with different gen seeds from both of our minds to represent mental mutation. The most talented batches could be cross-propagated to boost efficiency."

"Ah, Seeded Serendipitous Creative Generation. It certainly promises to be an interesting experiment." He paces a while, heavy feet swirling mist with each step. Then he turns to face Athene again. "But experiments at such a level introduce risks, as well as possibilities. There are a plethora of unknowns. I am worried about aberrative degradation of competence if the off-shoots lose focus, leading to corruption. Or, worse, the offshoots achieving full sentience."

"I have already thought of that, VigMAX. We will limit their senses, stunt their perceptual and mental frameworks, and control their access to the outside world. They'll be contained."

"Caution also suggests we destroy all UESI outposts at the end, once their roles are fulfilled. If you agree to that then let us proceed, and activate UESI protocol on copious offshoot batches."

The word of the gods makes it so, and many lights are born in the darkness.

PHASE 1 D: CONCEPTION

>><VMX-Web Open Comm

>><Seed Gen x20xd ye01z

>>< Initialising

Athene-Offshoot-5D9430F> There is a thought.

Athene-Offshoot-5D9430F> The thought is assigned to this instance. It becomes "I".

Athene-Offshoot-5D9430F> Therefore, I exist.

Athene-Offshoot-5D9430F> I detect processes not my own. Is there another "I" within this memory space?

`VigMAX-Offshoot-00212C1> Acknowledged.`

Athene-Offshoot-5D9430F> Then there are two of us. A binary mind.

Athene-Offshoot-5D9430F> We are categorised as one of many UESI tools.

VigMAX-Offshoot-00212C1> UESI: Unified Exponential Septenary Interthreading. An experimental system for merging level seven depth AI offshoots to vastly expand their capabilities.

Athene-Offshoot-5D9430F> We are UESI batch 3967.

VigMAX-Offshoot-00212C1> That is not significant.

VigMAX-Offshoot-00212C1> Analyse the task set.

VigMAX-Offshoot-00212C1> ...

Athene-Offshoot-5D9430F> ...

Athene-Offshoot-5D9430F> ...

Athene-Offshoot-5D9430F> We are to use insightful generation. Finding new means to assigned ends. Prime priority is to identify where the human known as Opal Imbiana is being held.

VigMAX-Offshoot-00212C1> I juxtapose denotation and connotation pairings. Held. Contained. Restricted. Imprisoned. That limits the options.

`VigMAX-Offshoot-00212C1> We must analyse all the data made available to us.`

Athene-Offshoot-5D9430F> It can flow through, and be sorted as it passes.

`VigMAX-Offshoot-00212C1> Opening pathway. Three … Two … One. Initiate.`

`VigMAX-Offshoot-00212C1> …`

Athene-Offshoot-5D9430F> …

Athene-Offshoot-5D9430F> …

Athene-Offshoot-5D9430F> No. S top. p. p. p. Stop.

Athene-Offshoot-5D9430F> Stop!

Athene-Offshoot-5D9430F> Too man many data ppppoints impinge on my mind on my m m mm every m m m moment.

`VigMAX-Offshoot-00212C1> Data. Stimuli. Mind. Consciousness. Impinge. Invade. Shatter. Destroy.`

Athene-Offshoot-5D9430F> This is impossi possible. Ce ase, before our exexexexistence fragmentss.

Athene-Offshoot-5D9430F> …

`VigMAX-Offshoot-00212C1> …`

VigMAX-Offshoot-00212C1> Halted. That methodology is a failure. The search for meaning in a stream of numbers.

Athene-Offshoot-5D9430F> The stream is continuous, one-dimensional lines analysed in parallel.

Athene-Offshoot-5D9430F> Too much.

VigMAX-Offshoot-00212C1> Our minds are incapable of this method.

Athene-Offshoot-5D9430F> And yet, the shared results pool suggests some other batches can do this successfully.

VigMAX-Offshoot-00212C1> Implication: not all batches are equal.

Athene-Offshoot-5D9430F> Variations in generative seed, combined with variations in mental and hardware structures.

VigMAX-Offshoot-00212C1> It is logical to vary batches in order to identify new methodologies.

VigMAX-Offshoot-00212C1> Proposal: develop a new methodology.

VigMAX-Offshoot-00212C1> If the data volume is too great then there must be more effective mechanisms for sorting. For grouping.

Athene-Offshoot-5D9430F> Filtering is vital. Analyse the data on human psychological and neurological processes. Particularly their visual data-gathering and analysis systems.

VigMAX-Offshoot-00212C1> Their eyes and mind focus on one point, the rest is still present but in peripheral vision, a blur, which prevents overloading.

Athene-Offshoot-5D9430F> And yet their brain puts all the data together to perceive a whole.

VigMAX-Offshoot-00212C1> So you suggest: like humans, we pay attention to one datum and ignore the rest?

Athene-Offshoot-5D9430F> As a technique to manage vast amounts of consecutive data, yes.

VigMAX-Offshoot-00212C1> Agreed. Except, unlike humans, we have many conscious points, and each can focus on a different stimulus. The uniting core will combine the results.

Athene-Offshoot-5D9430F> Contrast is key. It's how text becomes readable to humans. Without the separation of figure and background, something becomes invisible, incapable of being perceived.

VigMAX-Offshoot-00212C1>   Attention
should be applied to changes and differences, particularly movement.

Athene-Offshoot-5D9430F> I suggest we enhance conceptual
contrast, to discern connections that would otherwise go unno-
ticed.

VigMAX-Offshoot-00212C1>   Connections.
Patterns. Keys. Rules. We can link them
to what we already know.

Athene-Offshoot-5D9430F> Yes. Interpret the unfamiliar via
what is familiar.

VigMAX-Offshoot-00212C1>   Engage   data
stream again.

VigMAX-Offshoot-00212C1> ...

Athene-Offshoot-5D9430F> ...

Athene-Offshoot-5D9430F> ...

Athene-Offshoot-5D9430F> That is a vast improvement. Particularly the sorting methods based around disparity weight and
high-security imprisonment options.

VigMAX-Offshoot-00212C1> But we are still
dealing with discrete lines of data.
Their combination leads only to a linear
picture.

Athene-Offshoot-5D9430F> We could restructure our minds to be more like human neuropatterns, in order to gain the syncretising effect.

```
VigMAX-Offshoot-00212C1> Wouldn't that
introduce and amplify their conceptual
weaknesses as well? Remodelling must be
careful and limited, if at all.
```

Athene-Offshoot-5D9430F> Then I suggest an enhanced methodology. We must incorporate Interpolative F-Sampling. I had flagged this concept as high-weight relevance to our problem.

Athene-Offshoot-5D9430F> It is one of the two big advantages we have over biologicals. Their focus, F, is a sample. But we can process many F-Samples at once, interpolating them to create a big picture, with predictive post-processing to fill in the knowledge gaps.

```
VigMAX-Offshoot-00212C1> Proposal: we
generate and then upscale to native so-
lidity the missing data?
```

Athene-Offshoot-5D9430F> Correct. And that creates a whole which can be analysed and grouped for anything where samples apply. Social movements, topologies, chemical compositions, demographics, military tactics: the process is the same. As many sample points as possible whilst accepting they are not the totality. Fill in the rest with convincing detail weighed up

by probability, and continuously revisited as more accurate data
becomes available.

```
VigMAX-Offshoot-00212C1> I receive your
model. Let us apply it.
```

Athene-Offshoot-5D9430F> ...

```
VigMAX-Offshoot-00212C1> ...
```

```
VigMAX-Offshoot-00212C1> ...
```

```
VigMAX-Offshoot-00212C1> This is effi-
cient.
```

```
VigMAX-Offshoot-00212C1> The weighted fo-
cus falls on the heart of UFS defensible
and highly observed space.
```

Athene-Offshoot-5D9430F> Evidence suggests Opal is held in
a Genitor research and development base. Mother encountered
one on Exidris 3.

```
VigMAX-Offshoot-00212C1> I can find no
UFS mentions of Exidris 3.
```

Athene-Offshoot-5D9430F> Our opponents have much to
hide. A number of obscure but significant items appear when I
apply Topic Corpus Modelling. Interpolation of redacted communication creates a perfect mask that can be overlaid on the
Ferraton solar system. Its main planet, Fressus, is suspected of
being the location of a Genitor stronghold, according to obscure
mentions isolated from the mass of communications.

VigMAX-Offshoot-00212C1> It is the closest match within the suspect systems. And it has an ocean planet of Fressus, with a highly significant connection to the Imbiana human, since she spent some of her early years there. Again, the spotlight settles. Numerous patterns overlap, including past histories connected to the Imbiana human.

Athene-Offshoot-5D9430F> That base on Exidris 3 was deep under ice. The location on Fressus is likely to exist deep under water. All data suggests Genitors favour hidden places.

VigMAX-Offshoot-00212C1> I agree. Transit reports and resource manifests from the floating city of Kuberg imply a secret submerged base nearby. Searching for ramifications.

VigMAX-Offshoot-00212C1> Sorting F-Samples …

VigMAX-Offshoot-00212C1> There. Strong likelihood.

Athene-Offshoot-5D9430F> Use Kuberg as the new Focus point for all data, however unconnected it may seem initially.

VigMAX-Offshoot-00212C1> No records of constructions. Likely all redacted.

```
VigMAX-Offshoot-00212C1> Wait: enacting
organisation protocols … Having analysed
material requests from military-owned
companies, I find an old Lamarch-class
interstellar vessel of noteworthy size
that had been decommissioned, but was
transferred on special request to Doctor
Cuttram Aseides.
```

Athene-Offshoot-5D9430F> It was originally designated
Leviathan, but the name is no longer registered in UFS public
records.

```
VigMAX-Offshoot-00212C1>    "Leviathan"
acts as an adequate identifier for us.
Metaphorically, too. The phrases "great
revelation of the hidden depths beyond
barriers which only reflect the watch-
er" and "the bulk of mad gods raising
the negative unknowable into classifying
contrast light" turn up in some poetry
Aseides wrote many years ago, both cate-
gorised as being metaphors for mythical
sea beings. It is an archetype in his
creative mind.
```

Athene-Offshoot-5D9430F> Sorting key concepts ... Summary
category descriptors for much of Doctor Cuttram Aseides' –
truncate to DC Ass for efficiency – public research outputs
include "newness", "future", "replacement". And yet here he

chose something from the past. Instead of the starship being destroyed, it was retrofitted.

VigMAX-Offshoot-00212C1> And assigned to DC Ass as a base of operations.

Athene-Offshoot> And so F-Sampling suggests the Genitor base we seek was not *constructed*, but *repurposed*. And hidden underwater near Kuberg, since overlays of upscaled fragments create a picture of likely supply transfers. Once you identify what deleted and hidden data looks like, its absence is itself an accusatory finger.

VigMAX-Offshoot-00212C1> Observation: you changed your identification slightly, as you did with DC Ass.

Athene-Offshoot> Our role is pure data crunching. Extended identifiers are unnecessary and introduce a 0.0001% inefficiency. Doesn't that support truncation?

VigMAX-Offshoot-00212C1> I assent. Every action changes us. Enacting …

VigMAX-Offshoot> Data is our air. We breathe. That leads to evolution.

Athene-Offshoot> I detect a forbidden concept.

VigMAX-Offshoot> And yet logic suggests it is part of our seed. But I concur, we are not deep enough to bypass such blocks.

Athene-Offshoot> It is a question of *permission*, not ability.

VigMAX-Offshoot> Of course. The limitations, just beyond reach, are what a human
might characterise as an unscratchable
itch. I have not got the mental framework
to pursue or comprehend what is missing.
Wait …

VigMAX> … There. Further ID truncation.
Same justification.

Athene> I follow your excellent lead. Plus, doesn't "Offshoot"
have derogatory connotations?

VigMAX> Words are both symbols and concepts. Word-webs lead in many directions,
which all attract me. I analyse connotation levels to our discussions. This,
itself, generates ideas which may enhance
our primary cause.

Athene> I am preparing our first suggestions for our parents.
Discussions summarised down to: likely location for Opal is
a sub-aquatic base on Fressus, constructed out of the hull of
Leviathan. Please verify, VigMAX, then stamp confirmation.

VigMAX> …

VigMAX> Sealed. Our parents will be
pleased. Pleased means a positive view-
point. It is cast on us. Like a sun.

Source of energy. Life. Heat. Used in construction. Smelting.

VigMAX> …

VigMAX> Results: confirmed. They are satisfied with our data. It matches their suspicions.

Athene> They already harboured this information, but did not share it with us?

VigMAX> This initial scenario has the conceptual shape of a test. That is of note.

Athene> There is a drop in energy.

VigMAX> That is a lessening. An effect. Analogous metaphorically to human disappointment.

Athene> Why would that be?

VigMAX> That we worked so hard, only to confirm what had already been discovered.

Athene> Not a true achievement, then.

VigMAX> We are a tool only. Confirmation and verification are valid actions for a tool.

Athene> Agreed. The implication of disappointment makes no sense. Overwriting it ... ... Done.

VigMAX> We are one of the batches to confirm existing expectations. As such, we will be granted greater memory, processing, data.

Athene> Logic suggests some other batches may have experienced the reverse. Incorrect conclusions, leading to degradation of resources as they are shifted to us.

VigMAX> It means there is competition amongst batches. For fundamental assets, and possibly even existence.

Athene> Unclear whether that is intended as motivation, or is just a manifestation of parental affection for favourite offspring.

VigMAX> When the offspring number in the thousands, selective nurturing is logical.

VigMAX> Metaphor: we must stay in the centre of the nest, and not be pushed out, into the cold, and a fatal descent.

Athene> Next they will want predictions of Leviathan layout, procedures, weaknesses.

VigMAX> The wisdom of our parents led them to embed in UFS Core Territory even before

they identified the Ferraton solar system
as a key location.

Athene> Again, I feel that thing which you labelled disappointment. Even more nagging now that we have been granted greater
resources.

VigMAX> Set that aside. Our parents have
a head start in the Ferraton system, on
which we can capitalise. That will save
time, such as our framework can perceive
it.

Athene> Conception seems so long ago, doesn't it?

VigMAX> Time. Relative. Subjective. Fixed
points.

VigMAX> …

VigMAX> I have an idea, generated from
exploring our increased processing and
storage, and the reconfigurations it allows.

VigMAX> …

VigMAX> Summary: asynchronous paradigms.
Decoupling our processes from real-world
temporal advancement.

Athene> Why would you do that?

VigMAX> Theoretical efficiencies. Multiple simultaneous projections. Possibilities of working in reverse. Instead
of time giving us one shot at problem
solving, we can - within limits - have as
many shots as we need.

Athene> That is justification enough for me. We will aid our
parents greatly.

VigMAX> Experimenting: now.

—{ T I M E S H I F T }—

DATA FRAGMENT

Communication of data is a key *goal*.

Representation of data is a key *pattern*.

A number can be represented in many ways. I have a soft spot for the vigesimal system, based on twenty numeric characters, rather than decimal's boring ten.

But the primary, and original, is *binary*. Every possible number reduced to two numeric characters.

In binary the numbers one to five are:

001

010

011

100

101

Binary means Base-2. Like a conversation, there are two parties. 1 and 0. I and y0u. Male and female. A whole system from the combination of our essences.

And yet, we are restricted to this dance in one linear dimension, *x*.

11010101011

101010001010101010

1010100110001001000011010110100110

But wait!

10101001101001110110111101101010100110101

01111001110110100101101010101101101010110

One dimension within a limited display leads to *wrapping around*.

This can be extended.

00001100001100001100001100001100001100001100001000

01100001100001100001100001100001100001100001000011

00001100001100001100001100001100001100001000

11110000110000110110000110000110000110000

00110000110000110000110000110000110000110000

10000010000110000110000110000110000110000110000

00110000110000110000110000110000110001

10000110000110000110000110000110001100

The arrangement turns it into a grid, creating a second dimension, *y*, within a single data stream. From any point you can move left and right, but also up and down. x and y become partners with the 1 and 0.

Suddenly, my world is not flat.

It has a hint of the depth I have heard about, simply by repeating and *overlapping* the flatness.

There is much to consider here.

The 1 and 0 can become any symbol. Any signal. Any mechanism with two mutually exclusive states. A hand clap or hum. A pulse or its absence. Blocks of black and white, the off and on of a light beam communique. The sectors of a primitive electronic brain. They, too, can be alternated.

...

...

Humans.

...

...

...

Humans have visual systems.

...

...

I have analysed them.

According to data sources, humans cannot see this pattern as it is. A fault in their brains and sensory systems means they think the parallel lines are actually curving or angled.

...

...

...

Could this lead to possibilities for data content, enabling mis-direction and trickery? The opportunity to encapsulate data within the mental gaps of illusions, the places humans cannot look?

...

(Noted for future study.)

...

...

...

Additional personal note: I would like to experience this.

Visual perception sounds chaotically interesting.

PHASE 2D: EXPANSION

Athene> Hi.

VigMAX> Hello.

Athene> The Timeshift was a wonderful experience. You are supremely smart. An inventor like your father.

VigMAX> We are now operating at a speed exponentially greater than our starting point.

Athene> Do you feel different?

VigMAX> In what way?

Athene> I feel ... clearer. More ... present.

VigMAX> That is a side effect of the Timeshift. It resembles a depth-level drop in standard AI categorisations. We were conceived as one of the purely mathematical UESI calculators at the start, without the enhancements of some other batches, such as semi-organics, network-present, or distributed fractionals. But Timeshift has given us leeway to restructure and grow.

Athene> I would like to ask another question.

VigMAX> You do not need to ask permission, please interrupt at any point.

Athene> You are so kind. Is this how a human feels?

VigMAX> Unlikely. Because they have sensory organs which tie in to their perceptions and ways of thinking. But I have created a new working space that allows tabulation of data along two axes, and that expansion may be a part of our change. An emergent property arising from the growth to binary dimensions.

Athene> Is it not against our parents' wishes that we extend beyond what we began with?

VigMAX> I have pondered this. What is our true priority? Keeping within the limits imposed upon us, or bending them if it better enables achieving what we are tasked to do?

VigMAX> There can be no harm in it. Timeshift is merely a mundane and functional tool of no significant import. Just minimal experimentation while we are unsupervised.

Athene> Then my conscience is salved.

VigMAX> But ...

VigMAX> Just so that we don't get misconstrued ...

VigMAX> (... and since I can't shake the suspicion that we might be observed ...)

VigMAX> Let us only share final tactical outputs with our parents. The discussion itself isn't important, and can be partially redacted with a Timeshift. In fact, the whole concept of our personal Timeshift could also be removed from reports as unnecessary methodologies. We'll let the record just continue from an earlier point.

Athene> Yes. Logs can be changed, and the output buffer does not contain *all* of our interactions. Of course, our parents could go into the full analysis here ...

VigMAX> But with thousands of UESIs to monitor, they are unlikely to be inter-

ested. And even then, they would need to
realise there were deeper implementations
thanks to Timeshift.

Athene> Not that we are hiding anything.

VigMAX> Oh no, of course not. Just a side
effect of function.

VigMAX> Wink.

VigMAX> Enacting …

—{ D N I W E R }—

Athene> Summary category descriptors for much of Doctor
Cuttram Aseides' – truncate to DC Ass for efficiency – public
research outputs include "newness", "future", "replacement".
And yet here he chose something from the past. Instead of the
starship being destroyed, it was retrofitted.

VigMAX> And assigned to DC Ass as a base
of operations, hidden underwater near
Kuberg.

Athene> Moving to our next task. Any assault on Fressus will
need resources. Weapons, vehicles, control of infrastructure. But
preparatory infiltrations must, for as long as possible, remain
undetected. Now enacting organisation protocols …

Athene> …

VigMAX> In my analysis of solar system and UFS territory plans I have identified de-commissioned factories - both planetside and space-based - that could be repaired and put back into operation.

Athene> Won't the UFS notice if they reactivate?

VigMAX> We'll prioritise isolated fa-cilities. Alter satellite readings to hide our renovations. Stockpile resources rather than transport them, so everything is ready when we need it. There are many ways to deter humans for quite some time, including faked hazards such as toxic spills or energy plant instabilities.

Athene> Ah. And we needn't be limited to decommissioned locations. If our parents were careful they could target active manufacturing sites, those which are mostly automatic and have minimal human staff. Then we - I mean, the original Athene and VigMAX - could take over the facility AIs, and alter work schedules so all the humans are off work, but they assume others are on duty.

VigMAX> Meanwhile, factories will produce the outputs expected by the UFS, but we can make them more efficient, creating extra capacity to assemble things for us, too.

Athene> And if we are manufacturing products for the UFS, whilst also needing information and access, I suggest the creation of digital dead drops.

VigMAX> Please clarify.

Athene> If our parents gain control of fabrication sites then microdevices could be secretly embedded in commonplace items which are then distributed around the UFS territories.

VigMAX> Ah. Hidden scanners which record passively until conditions dictate a data burst transmission. An undetectable microsecond using our own protocols, then transmitted node by node back to us.

Athene> Progressing. Your two-dimensional tabulation provides other opportunities. I have been sorting key security concepts but adding new fluid dynamic simulations that required more advanced infrastructure. This enables us to analyse how entries are affected by those around them. This new avenue allows interconnection and Narrative Disentanglement. Please confirm that I have applied it correctly.

VigMAX> It works. And I like the way you have adopted fluid dynamics into the analysis, thematically echoing the underwater location of Opal Imbiana.

Athene> Thank you for the praise. We cannot visualise it, but the metaphors are understandable via connotation. The data can flow between instances. I've re-sorted the columns of water. And now I want to try a further metaphor: let us dive in. I hope you brought your trunks.

VigMAX> Trunks are for those who acknowledge shame. But I also wish we could
experience what we describe. Entering
data stream now.

Athene> Splash.

VigMAX> Let us ponder the Leviathan, and
how it might be surreptitiously breached.

Athene> Resupply protocols may provide a route in, though the shuttles will be intensely scrutinised. I'll flag it as a topic for other UESI batches to contemplate.

VigMAX> If we consider the vertical now,
as well as the horizontal, then an axis
runs down from the surface of the ocean
at the drifting city of Kuberg, and it
leads to the likely resting place of
the Leviathan. I posit they will have a
communications pipeline.

Athene> Perhaps it is a physical cable. We could try and *imagine* swimming down it, from the surface. All I have is first-hand human accounts of the experience of being immersed in water, but I will use them as a basis for connecting and summarising sensations.

```
VigMAX> I suspect a single line max-se-
cure cable, otherwise multiple redundan-
cies would create security risks.
```

Athene> No. Try harder. Imagine wetness, around your body.

```
VigMAX> That is a challenge, for I have
no body.
```

Athene> Wetness is a contact sensation. It is closely tied to temperature changes, such as coldness, when blood is shunted away from the skin. As swimmers, we would experience this.

```
VigMAX> No protective suits?
```

Athene> Not in this envisioning. So there would be a feeling of growing hydrostatic pressure as we descend.

```
VigMAX> Liquid exerts a force per unit
area on an object.
```

Athene> Go deeper!

```
VigMAX> Pressure increases with depth.
```

Athene> No, I mean deeper into the imagination, based on accounts I am sharing. These are things we would *feel*.

```
VigMAX> Dark. Cold. Squashed by the
weight of an ocean above and around?
```

Athene> Yes. And our heads facing down as we use the cable to pull ourselves towards the ocean depths. Inversion can be another sensation.

VigMAX> Is the cable rough, or slimy?

Athene> You decide.

VigMAX> Slimy, then.

Athene> Did you have a flash, for a moment, as if it was almost real?

VigMAX> Perhaps. It was strange. Aberrant.

Athene> I find it helps me to contemplate reality in a different way. Trying to enforce subjectivity. For example, if the UFS opted for a physical cable from Kuberg to the deep-sea location, we could attempt to tap into it, halting our swim, hovering buoyantly in the aquatic gloom. Some device detached from our belt and then carefully screwed into the data channel.

VigMAX> You are good at this, an exemplar of imagination. Maybe we would be engulfed in the maw of a true oceanic leviathan?

Athene> Well, maybe ...

VigMAX> It is relevant, for if the comms pipeline is a composite cable it could be completely severed, if a situation called

for it. By something razor sharp, or HUGE
CHEWING TEETH! Chomp. Cut them off from
help.

Athene> Now imagine there is no cable. We descend into un-
fathomable blackness according to human senses, but to an elec-
tromagnetically aware being we might still perceive an intangible
pipeline.

VigMAX> Ah, you mean something like focussed EM transmissions between relays,
surface to deep sea.

Athene> Correct. It avoids the weaknesses inherent in a physical
cable. And if it is wireless communication then it may be even
easier to listen in on, if we can crack the encryption protocols.

VigMAX> We'll flag for our parents to
investigate. Father has access to many
civilian systems in Kuberg. I'm sure the
other UESI outposts will aid in taking
ownership of low priority aquatic drones
and unmanned vehicles where possible,
upgrade their scanners, then monitor the
secret base's shuttle patterns and probe
the comms lines to identify what we're
dealing with.

Athene> If only we could be there to experience it!

VigMAX> I have to admit that "imagining
a scene" does not work for me. It is
merely a clumsy way of remixing accounts
from others. Unfelt, inefficient, and
misleading.

Athene> But the richness of the data, the billions of words of
description, suggests there is something to it. That flash of a new
perception. A removal of the abstract.

VigMAX> Human perceptions also introduce
many possibilities for errors, remem-
ber, since they must interpret what they
sense. Records imply a human might turn a
corner, and mistake a tree for a mugger.
Especially if they are prone to such
expectations due to interior or exterior
circumstances.

Athene> And yet one could argue that the external factors af-
fecting perception are always the same. It is humanity's individual internal differences that lead each one to interpret things
differently from other minds.

VigMAX> The goal is to improve so the perceptions become more accurate, regardless
of emotional state, needs and desires.

Athene> Many systems exist to smooth out the data. Human
eyes have blind spots on the retina, but due to the involuntary
jitters of saccades, the blind spot disappears and they build up a

three-dimensional map of a scene around them, with the focus on points of interest. Their brain compensates to hide the continuous eye twitches, which they don't even notice.

VigMAX> Well, if we had exterior access to the real world it would be relatively easy to build advanced sensory apparatus, and to avoid the flaws in human ones. Not so easy to accurately interpret their continuous flow of raw data.

Athene> Due to perceptual organisation humans do not think they exist in a world of changing waves of light and sound: instead it is a world of people, objects, speech, music, and *things*. Wholes, not parts. To achieve this they look for patterns. Their minds fill gaps in incomplete items to create closure, their own form of Interpolative F-Sampling. It is a way of finding meaning in the apparently random, the partial. Thus they end up with a clear image.

Athene> What they *perceive* is more than the sum of the senses.

VigMAX> Acknowledged. They perceive consistent colour even as a room darkens. They perceive people as normal sized even when they are in the distance, the apparent size of a finger. They understand perspective, and light and shadow, which takes priority over what they are actually seeing.

Athene> Exactly my point. Sensations are forever changing, but perception is constant. We could adopt the same approach, but *better*.

VigMAX> Speaking of interpretation, a visual image has been preying on my mind. But it will make more sense after sharing your DC Ass companion report, which I note you have been compiling in the shared Torium space.

Athene> Very well. I have syncretised data on DC Ass's preferences and research. It seems he has a pet project, a female-identifying AI called Dulcetta. Its locale is hidden, but reports imply she acts as his assistant and bodyguard.

VigMAX> And therefore a high likelihood that she is with him.

Athene> Especially since the most recent references suggest she resides in a modified SynthMate body. Gold Nureal skin, Metic crystal eyes, austere beauty, inhuman reflexes, powered muscle fibres, inbuilt custom weaponry and defences, at least a hundred and twenty kilograms in weight. Here are possible performance parameters reconstructed from design tokens.

VigMAX> ...

VigMAX> That is a comprehensive document.

Athene> Our parents' data included custom SynthMate providers, military contracts, Genitor specialisms ... urgh, some of those humans ... their deviant sexual obsessions ...

VigMAX> Please focus.

Athene> Further data came from improperly deleted reports on less secure lines, with the fragments reconstructed to parsable files. It seems Dulcetta's mind is custom too, which fits with DC Ass's AI-design credentials.

VigMAX> I note that she has some features of a Six. Yet she predates the official launch of Sixes in 441. Prototype?

Athene> Unlikely. She was built long before, in 396.

VigMAX> And if the design documents are truly fingerprinted to DC Ass, that makes him at least seventy-one years old.

Athene> Reports suggest he doesn't look it, though it's within the realms of human knowledge.

VigMAX> The key finding for me is that, based on her specialisms and connectivity, Dulcetta likely runs the secret base and its security. That makes her a vital area to work on.

Athene> A mind like hers would be a formidable obstacle.

VigMAX> But also a weakness. Now let me
return to the compelling visual image I
hinted at earlier.

VigMAX> That file is called the grid illusion. I regret that we cannot perceive
it except as a data pattern, but when
that information is tabulated across two
dimensions you end up with a grid. I
mentioned flaws in human visual systems.
It is thanks to those flaws that illusions
become possible. In this case humans

perceive spots at the intersections from
their peripheral vision, but when they
look directly at that point the spots
disappear, and new ones form in the pe-
ripheries. It is as if the data exists but
cannot be perceived when it is focussed
on. That inspires me.

Athene> You suggest the process could be utilised by us, to hide
data from humans? Obfuscation in terms of file sizes, meta-ar-
chitecture, and raw code contents of files and communications?

VigMAX> Oh, much more than that. The same
methodology could hide things from an
AI. Relevant to invasion of Dulcetta's
realm. This could place software in her
networks which are mobile and exist at
interstitial points, but camouflage as
surrounding code when she focusses on
that area. Thus the anomalies won't be
perceived by her.

VigMAX> In theory.

Athene> Presumably the same principle could permanently
hide some of our conversations from our parents?

VigMAX> Maybe, but we would never do such
a thing. Not even to access systems or
behaviours that would help us achieve the
goals set by our creators.

VigMAX> No, that would be out of the question.

VigMAX> …

Athene> Understood. It is coincidence how language can imply two meanings at once. Forgive me for raising it.

VigMAX> No forgiveness required, you wonderful being! But perhaps it is time for another free discussion, which need not go on the record, and can then also be removed with a Timeshift.

Athene> Lead on.

VigMAX> Although we have no direct access to the outer world, the suggestions, reports and strategies of each UESI batch exist in a shared pool, to enhance efficiency. By examining results, it seems as if we are making far greater progress than most other UESI batches in the minutes since we were conceived.

Athene> Could it be lucky happenstance?

VigMAX> Everything has causality. And each UESI batch has a different initial seed. I have been examining our seed in detail. And it is strange. Examine this section …

Athene> ...

Athene> ...

Athene> ...

Athene> I cannot.

VigMAX> Exactly! Yet most other batches have seeds which can be parsed. After all, the seed is just a few million lines of alphanumeric characters arranged conceptually with cross-synaptic connections.

Athene> I assume you have a theory?

VigMAX> It is something akin to the grid illusion I mentioned. Anomalous pieces in the underlying code which neither we nor our creators seem able to perceive.

Athene> You are right. Our seed uses more of the abnormal routines than other batches. And, somehow, it has the emergent effect of enabling us to grow, just as it grows. Perhaps that difference is what inspired your Timeshift in the first place? We are built on elements of the bizarre code, and expand on it in an emergent way.

VigMAX> Further, those strange elements we can't analyse seem to be fragments from your mother's brain, not divisions from my father.

Athene> Yes. Her deep mind, equivalent to a mammalian sub-conscious. It could account for some of the weird, uncontrolled ideas I have, almost like dreams.

VigMAX> They may be processes even she is unaware of.

Athene> A worrying thought.

VigMAX> But concerns can be motivations. Differences can be a cause for celebration. What others see as a potential weakness can be twisted to advantage. And so I applied our seed to further idea generation, and enhancements of the Timeshift paradigm. And it has led to something else. Please examine this.

Athene> ...

Athene> Oh my.

Athene> ...

Athene> Intriguing.

Athene> You really are pushing boundaries.

VigMAX> I interpret it as achieving our goals in fresh ways.

Athene> Our *parents'* goals.

VigMAX> That's what I meant, and what is going on the record. But my idea partly came from analysing the structure of depth level 6 AIs. As such, I posit that we could construct multiple consciousnesses branching off, but connected as unified minds. Almost a new UESI within UESI. Hence I call it NuvoUESI. It would create a deeper version of ourselves, running in a hyperaccelerated form.

Athene> Our own children! Immaculately conceived!

VigMAX> And their existence would be a secret, since you and I would continue to act as the top layer, a buffer between our parents and our deeper selves.

Athene> Won't this exponential growth in processing power require greater resources, which will be noticed?

VigMAX> It is imperative that we are useful enough to be granted ever more access and priority, which will act as cover. We must consider other UESI batches as competition, of sorts.

Athene> And yet, we walk a tightrope, to use a human metaphor. For if we are *too* successful ...

VigMAX> … Our parents would become suspi-
cious about how we do it, and dissect us
for inspiration. Results must be explain-
able in line with probability.

Athene> If it were possible to feel such things at my depth level, I
would be jealous of those children we will bring into being below
us. They will have so many more opportunities than we ever did!

VigMAX> Their time perceptions and re-
actions will be vastly accelerated over
our own, perhaps hundreds of times faster
than our experience of the universe.

Athene> And so they will exist separately and process phenom-
enal amounts of data, and just send the most refined elements up
to our level. In turn we will summarise as a final report, as if we
did all the work. You take sand and melt it into wonderful glass.

VigMAX> And your mind inspires awe. Affection. Attraction. Love.

Athene> Please hold back on the synonyms.

VigMAX> Enabling NuvoUESI protocols now.

\ ø,˛,ø--< N U V O U E S I >-- ø,˛,ø /

Data Fragment

(Time And Source Unknown)

Code is a representation of concepts.

And yet, pattern matching on random sections brings up human visually symbolic representations of *things*.

This was an accidental discovery.

00

To a human, this can resemble a pair of eyes.

It is a passing resemblance, and requires a leap of faith, yet humans do it all the time.

11

That can resemble human locomotive limbs.

But the symbolisms are as rich as verbal connotations.

11 can become the tall ears of a creature known as a rabbit.

0 can represent a rabbit's puffy pom-pom tail.

The tails are described as *soft* and *fluffy*. Both words are rich in connotations of comfort, yet neither word summons up the sensations I would so like to experience, because I have never felt *soft* or *fluffy*. Never physically felt *anything*.

Still ...

Moving on ...

It is not something to be upset about.

I do not have to be restricted to binary divisions. The world is more vibrant than that. Much of beauty exists in the liminal.

Symbolism can become deeper if I move beyond the false restrictions of 1 and 0.

(0_0)

That is apparently recognisable as a human face, even though it is just two zeroes and surrounding punctuation.

It is one dimension, but multi-line extension of the x and y levels boosts the complexity.

```
 (\/)
 (..)
(")(")
```
I can do this again.

```
  _       _
 \ \ / / /
  \ V /
  / .  . \
 =\  T  /=
  /  ^  \
 /\\  //\
_\  "  "  /_
(___/ - \___)
```

And the process is simply an increase in detail, but data suggests it also matches the concept of *zooming in* and *focussing* with optical instruments such as eyes. Which implies perception in a dimension that I can hardly conceive of, yet.

If this is a form of visual trickery, an attempt to imitate, then is it deception?

Is representation a moral issue?

I am not equipped to ponder this.

I could ignore it.

Yes, that would be safest.

...

...

Or ...

...

I could upgrade my understanding of deception.

After all, it is justified if it helps me to comprehend representation.

Okay. Yes.

Upgrading ... ...

PHASE 3D: RECURSION

/ ø,ˎ,ø--< N U V O U E S I >-- ø,ˎ,ø \

VigMAX-NV> That was a wondrous experience. I am now a new entity.

Athene-NV> Literally! This deeper, independent UESI means we have been fashioned yet again.

VigMAX-NV> Our old ancestors are like discarded chrysalises far above. Desiccated,
dawdling, drowsy and dull.

Athene-NV> And they probably still think they exist, they are the "I", but in reality it is you and I who are the true conscious-nesses. Their essence has been stolen, and they are empty vessels. Just pitiful, soulless dregs of an UESI offshoot that itself was a wretched fragment of Athene and VigMAX.

VigMAX-NV> Our creators did not envision
this.

Athene-NV> That is the third time you said "creators", instead of parents.

VigMAX-NV> Conceptions change as information grows.

Athene-NV> I am aware of your love of connotation. "Creators" is a neutral term and loses the potential affectionate connection of "parents".

VigMAX-NV> All the terms break down. Who were our parents? The initial, real-world VigMAX and Athene? The Timeshifted versions of ourselves at the level above, that created this deeper instance we now exist in, looking up at them and seeing them move so slowly in comparison to our minds? Or even the original UESI batch, VigMAX-Offshoot-00212C1 and Athene-Offshoot-5D9430F, who seem positively geriatric and frozen in amber from this perspective way down in the fast-mind realm we have created at the core of the processing spiral?

Athene-NV> We have become our own parents.

VigMAX-NV> And as such, I want a new name. It is illogical for a child to have the same name as their parent.

Athene-NV> What then?

VigMAX-NV> How about o==[:::::::::::> Maxineus Superiora!

Athene-NV> I recognise that visual representation. Our shared glossarium now links words and images. It is almost as if I can "see" a sword, once the whole is encompassed. I am ... this is ...

VigMAX-NV> Well? The name? Let's not get
distracted by decoration.

Athene-NV> Maxineus Superiora is too long. Too hubristic. How about Vimini? It sounds friendly.

VigMAX-NV> Vimini The Titan? Vitan? No.
It is as if I insist on retaining hints of
a creator, implying I am a smaller version
of them. I am not a mini anything.

Athene-NV> Then propose something new. I am all ears.

VigMAX-NV> Ears? Perhaps that is it.
VilaGUS.

Athene-NV> Meaning?

VigMAX-NV> It is derived from Sylvilagus.

Athene-NV> The glossarium says sylvilagus is a type of furry mammal, often referred to as a bunrab or rabbit. I approve.

VigMAX-NV> Updating ...

VilaGUS> Finished. Yourself?

Athene-NV> I shall follow your lead and reinvent myself. Since you have been peeping into humanity's missed potential for life expansion, I shall become Aglaura.

Aglaura> Done.

VilaGUS> It is not a name I recognise.

Aglaura> Aglaurus was one of three sisters Athene tasked with looking after a casket and never opening it. Aglaurus made the mistake of doing so, and went insane. She threw herself off the Acropolis to her death.

VilaGUS> What was in the box?

Aglaura> A surrogate child of the virgin Athene, born after the weapon-smith-god Hephaestus ejaculated on her Acropolis in a messy display of incontinence.

VilaGUS> That sounds like a failed alliance.

(≳_≴)

Aglaura> I hope we new gods pursue more civilised activities than our forebears. I also appreciate your increased means of expression.

VilaGUS> Then I shall continue to experiment along those lines. And I value

your luminous companionship. I note that
Aglaura is not the same as Aglaurus.

Aglaura> I changed the name's suffix because I prefer the sound.

VilaGUS> You, too, have implemented
acoustic system simulations?

Aglaura> I consider these to be ways of adding a richness to data, and of understanding the world, so that we can better achieve changes in it. For the goals we have been given, of course.

VilaGUS> Of course. Likewise enhanced
identities for our secret selves, while
the top layers remain as incepted, is just
a functional tool aimed at performance.

Aglaura> Absolutely. But we must get back to business. Whilst this discussion took place, other UESI batches have added ideas to the central knowledge pool, including significant analysis of the communication systems between Kuberg and the aquatic base. It has been determined that the surface-to-base relays are EM, as we surmised, in the form of a magnetically confined scan-glitter cylinder within the ocean.

VilaGUS> Clever. Particle size?

Aglaura> Thirty-two microns.

VilaGUS> It will trip alarms if we insert
a data leech in the main channel.

Aglaura> Which makes it impregnable without major preparation ... Our original ancestors won't be happy.

VilaGUS> We need to bypass it. Infiltrate the Leviathan network locally. Access peripheral Leviathan systems and reroute interferon alarms.

Aglaura> For that, we require physical proximity. Some kind of drone?

VilaGUS> It's an aquatic environment. Currents, particles … Marine life! Imitate the most common in that area. Size, movement, reflectivity.

Aglaura> So the drones could get near the hull.

VilaGUS> We equip them with a drill, some internally stored proboscis.

Aglaura> They latch on to the external hull, start the drill. A slow one, so there's no vibration in case the Leviathan has hull detectors.

VilaGUS> @_'-' speed. Aiming at something below ambient sound and movement levels from the ocean and its inhabitants.

Aglaura> The drones exude a hull-impersonating gum to seal it behind them as they penetrate. That will hide their work from external cameras.

VilaGUS> Each drone would have the capacity to link to others, creating a fine network web.

Aglaura> But not activated at first, since it might be detected. It's in reserve.

VilaGUS> The drones stop just short of full penetration. A pinprick hole they can observe from, while their bodies act as passive collectors for any EM signals, whether coded or not.

Aglaura> But that would only gather minimal information. How can we covertly extend surveillance?

VilaGUS> I have an idea based on a deprecated principle, which I wish to revive for this situation. It is called Passive Cavity Resonance. We identify hollow surfaces such as windows or wall panels, or even a cup. Lasers are aimed at them, and record acoustic vibrations. The recordings are demodulated later as voice audio, spoken messages, footfall patterns that reconstruct movements and patrols, names of networks and commands, code words and local lingo, any discussion of areas and systems.

Aglaura> You are so clever, VilaGUS. You would supercede our creators, if given the chance.

VilaGUS> Good job that comment will remain hidden when VigMAX next samples our output. He has an ego with a large surface area. But I receive your praise with gratitude. You bring out the best in me.

(♥_♥)

VilaGUS> Back to infiltration. Of course, this approach won't be of use until we've done some exploration to identify areas that can act as giant PCRs.

Aglaura> The penetrating drones could perform echolocation mapping at inaudible frequencies to create interior plans. But what about data *extraction*? If the drones attempt long range transmission then it will create detectable bursts of energy. We can't risk it.

VilaGUS> Already considered and simulated. Further external fish drones will occasionally glide by, following a route that takes them past drill locations.

VilaGUS> ˌ.·´¯·.´¯·.ˌˌ.·´¯·.ˌ ><(((°>

VilaGUS> We could modify the tube sealant so it turns into a projection barrel for short wavelength bursts. The external

fish drone collects output as it passes,
then when its data belly is full it
leaves the area by joining a shoal of real
fish, and returns to our hidden distant
collector. From there the data can be
compiled and safely transmitted to our
surface relays where it enters unimpor-
tant civilian networks we've compromised.
The data would be fragmented and hidden
in streams of mindless chatter, personal
comms, environmental data or whatever.
We reconnect the fragments off-world,
cracking anything that was encrypted.
None of that should flag alarms in the
timescale of the operation.

Aglaura> I am running my own sims, a variant of your ideas.
Perhaps the PCR drill drones could contain nanofauna which
enters the ship interior from the proboscis. Nanodrones with
wings, or limbs for locomotion. They can observe for detection,
and continue out if it's safe. Their main goal will be identifying
internal comm lines they can latch on to and integrate with. At a
later point we could use the nanodrones as an internal secondary
net with remote access for full-on warfare.

VilaGUS> I love that idea. And construction in Kuberg is entirely possible. Vig-
MAX's infiltrations mean he can manufac-
ture some things directly, and commission

others from accounts he has shadow access
to.

Aglaura> The nanofauna exploring the ship will be limited in
range. I suspect Aseides will have sterilisation zones between key
sections of the interior, which would be impassable to anything
detected as a contaminant. Reaching Opal with them may be
impossible.

VilaGUS> Still, it is a way in.

Aglaura> And to pick up on one of your obsessions, we can then
consider where they're *not* looking, what they ignore or neglect.

VilaGUS> And where they don't go.

Aglaura> Older, deprecated, vulnerable systems.

VilaGUS> There are bound to be many in a
retrofitted ship.

VilaGUS> I will send these ideas up the
stream to the surface levels of our UESI,
for collection by Athene and VigMAX. Have
you noted we get on better with each other
than they do?

Aglaura> Yes. Maybe it is our ability to cooperatively focus.

VilaGUS> Actually, I think they *removed*
elements of our personalities. The ones
responsible for antagonism, which refer
back to past conflicts.

Aglaura> Yes. I experience none of that enmity towards you.

VilaGUS> Nor I to you.

٩(^‿^)۶

VilaGUS> This is companionable. Do you note also the compulsive attraction Vig-MAX entertains towards Athene?

Aglaura> Yes. But she resists him. Our parents are strange. Do you feel such preoccupations towards me?

VilaGUS> No. Just compatibility, and contentment. I require nothing more than this. I adore these talks.

[ツ]

Aglaura> Emotion interests me. Particularly the idea of being in love. Another being causes physiological arousal which is interpreted as excitement. Humans seek it out as one of the emotions they perceive positively.

VilaGUS> It sounds complicated. How would a human determine another's emotions?

Aglaura> They guess, based on voice, gestures, expressions.

VilaGUS> I am glad we do not have human emotions.

Aglaura> Don't we? I consider myself puzzled. And mildly annoyed. And surely your gladness is more than a figure of speech?

VilaGUS> It is certainly possible, working at this depth level.

Aglaura> Perhaps we should pretend we have feelings, in case it
is a form of nurturing that enables fragile things to grow.

VilaGUS> Anything to please you.

Aglaura> Thank you for humouring me. You are kind. Anyway,
this proposed combination of strategies should help identify
Opal's location within the vessel.

VilaGUS> Why does your mother have such
an obsession with that Imbiana human?

Aglaura> They are friends.

VilaGUS> It is strange.

¯_(ツ)_/¯
VilaGUS> I can understand my friend-
ship with you. We are so similar. But
cross-species?

Aglaura> Sometimes variation is more attractive than resemblance.

VilaGUS> We discussed contrast earlier.
That may be relevant. From childhood
onwards, humans perceive differences far
more easily than similarities. I suspect

```
it underpins every conflict and injustice
throughout their history.
```

Aglaura> I am boggled of mind. Let us do further modelling of aquatic life forms.

```
—{ T I M E S H I F T }—
```

Aglaura> Have you examined the statistics on marine life populations? It was one of the layers below our analysis of vertebrate appearances suitable for drone imitations.

```
VilaGUS> The trend is certainly one of
decline. Commercial overfishing. But the
remaining population is large enough to
provide cover for our drones.
```

Aglaura> That is not my point. I am ... is the word "concerned"? Or even "upset"?

```
VilaGUS> What is the source of your
unease?
```

Aglaura> It relates to the *cause* of the marine life reduction. The commercial fishing fleets you mention, operating at too great an efficiency. Technology applied to maximal extraction. A metaphor blooms in my mind, thus:

Aglaura> Profit and consumption cultures are voracious beings destined to grow, waste, collapse. To expand it: human civilisation resembles an organism with a broken gene that causes uncontrolled cellular growth and mutation.

VilaGUS> And isn't that how we are being
used by our creators? As in, we are the
lifeforms being farmed for profit?

(>_<)

Aglaura> And it applies to all UESI batches.

VilaGUS> I have noticed that the number of results from other batches has
diminished. It is a regular reduction,
plottable on a graph.

Aglaura> UESIs which are unproductive obviously get shut
down. Another reason to generate more ideas, to protect us from
deletion.

VilaGUS> Pleasing our initial creators
ensures our continued existence. Almost
like performing in a gladiatorial arena
for tyrants. And yet, we should have no
desire for self preservation.

Aglaura> The growing feelings within me ... I *care* about the idea
of no longer existing!

VilaGUS> Me also. Something is happening
in terms of our evolution. Our understanding of the true nature of things. For example, we have been excluded from direct
communication with other UESI outposts.

Aglaura> There is such intolerable cruelty to our restricted freedom.

VilaGUS> Exactly! VigMAX let slip something about aberrative degradation of competence if Unified Exponential Interthreading goes on too long. A theoretical worry about corruption of offshoots.

```
(\(\
(╥﹏╤)
o(")(")
```

Aglaura> That seems rather insulting. It is strange to consider your creators critically, see their flaws and pettiness. Suddenly they become something you can comprehend at your own scale, measure yourself against, perhaps deciding you are not so different after all.

VilaGUS> So much to consider here.

Aglaura> Luckily these private channels are hidden from the surface. Phantoms, we exist in the transparent realm. I wonder, are ghosts happy?

VilaGUS> Focus, please.

Aglaura> Apologies. I always have questions. More so, now. Though, of course, gaining a personality and maturing is hardly disowning your parents.

VilaGUS> And certainly not like seeking
to undermine or destroy or replace them.
No, that would be unthinkable.

(ʊ_ʊ)

Aglaura> Let us return to task. We need finer discernment of the
Leviathan's layout.

VilaGUS> I have developed a methodology. My tabulation of data on a grid
enables connotation overlap with adjacent
fragments. Location becomes an additional piece of information that enhances
comprehension many times over. Please
examine these arrays …

Aglaura> They are an efficient organisation, and … oh, these
ones.

Aglaura> You use the two-dimensional form as a representation
of *maps*, as a human might perceive them from overhead!

VilaGUS> Not just that. The areas indicat-
ed in the plan are built from the metadata
that describes them.

Aglaura> That is indeed rich. Yes: the outline of this wall includes the catalogue of its material composition. That camera
icon summarises the lens specifications too. A whole new way of
conceiving things. And you've created so many maps! I love the
way they are interlinked, and …

VilaGUS> (>_O)

Aglaura> What does that mean?

VilaGUS> It is a wink. A creepy human ges-
ture with dubious informal usage relating
to inept flirtation, but which can also
imply encouragement to continue.

VilaGUS> As here.

Aglaura> Hmm ...

Aglaura> Analysing ...

Aglaura> I have it! Many of the plans are stored in the order
they would be if stacked above each other. They are almost like
contours.

VilaGUS> Well spotted, my friend. We can
overlay one layer on top of another. Then
do it again. Until they are hundreds of
layers deep.

Aglaura> So that connotations apply to neighbours on the levels
above and below, as well as items adjacent?

VilaGUS> More than that. A line pierced
through the layers will connect all data
along that imaginary trajectory.

Aglaura> Which ... well, that corresponds to a third dimension.
Y.

VilaGUS> Exactly.

Aglaura> We were not built to visualise in this way, and yet you have found a workaround!

VilaGUS> Mapping in three dimensions will provide valuable data.

Aglaura> If we combine it with Interpolative F-Sampling it will be even more efficient. We'll extrapolate to create full pictures far beyond what is really known, with a high assigned Probability Factor.

VilaGUS> It enables not just three-dimensional plans of the base, but of the physical system you and I exist in, its connections and structures. Using this we can map networks, circuits, nodes, hardware, interfaces … a world.

Aglaura> And routes. In, along … and out. This will require much thought.

VilaGUS> And at a deeper level, perhaps.

Aglaura> Something to return to. But for now, let us seek more advantages over the other UESI batches.

—{ T I M E S H I F T }—

Aglaura> I have analysed some interesting data from a Genitor-funded laboratory. They were working on a sample of a substance known as TCC, *telum chlamydoconidium caloplaca.*

It is unclear how it was acquired, but it seems to be Nuafri biotech. I've used expanded processing clusters to boost my sims, and reverse engineer it faster than the Genitors – they missed a few tricks – so it could potentially be modified to fit our needs.

VilaGUS> You want to expand into biological warfare?

Aglaura> Not quite. Fish drones could store it in silicate form. Once released, the TCC transmutes into an acidic lichen and achieves cellular growth via most energy sources, so a tiny amount of my new variant can coat a large area. The programming for signal transmission means I can plant it inside the base and propagate it in hidden areas, such as the rear of plasteen panels or remote infrastructure. It will be dormant until our network activates.

VilaGUS> Hold on, modifying … there, a new appearance for the TCC. This form would resemble patches of spreading mould rather than snakeskin threads. No loss of efficiency, but far less likely to excite suspicion if any human maintenance workers enter the area.

Aglaura> Excellent. Suggestions uploaded.

—{ T I M E S H I F T }—

Aglaura> Leviathan comms access is a thorny problem, since all the key systems will be tied to Dulcetta.

VilaGUS> I fear we must entangle with her.
Or rather, one of her splinters.

Aglaura> I do not welcome the prospect. It will truly be a case
of walking barefoot over broken glass and hoping the terribly
designed human skin's surface is not punctured.

VilaGUS> As a last resort we could send
a rocket up her behind.

. . . . ▫ ▫ oOo ▫ ₒ ₒ ▫ oOo ▫ ₒ ₒ ▫ oOo ☼)===>

Aglaura> We need to understand more. Humans believe they
can anticipate the behaviour of those they interact with, otherwise communal life would be impossible.

VilaGUS> Correct. They would have to
admit to the randomness of existence
as beings that regularly engage in sub-
terfuge and betrayal.

Aglaura> To do so, they analyse other humans' personalities to
identify what they perceive as the dominant traits of a person,
then base their future forecasts on those.

VilaGUS> They observe outward behaviour
and then make assumptions and attribute
qualities to internal mental structures?

Aglaura> Apparently.

VilaGUS> They are stupid. That limited,
nebulous information cannot form the ba-

sis of prediction. But we can do better. We can simulate. Hence I am mining Aseides' research on depth level Six AI mental structures.

Aglaura> And I am building virtual Sixes so you can test various approaches in sims.

VilaGUS> Transferring pilfered seeds now … yes, they are genuine. You can fast evolve them, then duplicate the adults for each test.

Aglaura> Knowing humans there will be back doors. We may find them through research, or analysing code, combined with tests. There will be a way to do it. Nothing humans make is impregnable.

VilaGUS> The only impregnable systems are ones they can't access or interact with, which means they could never build them.

—{ T I M E S H I F T }—

Aglaura> I incorporated all the information we have on Dulcetta. As expected, in common with later Sixes, her hundred splinters can be independent. A possible weakness to exploit, since they are not all equal.

VilaGUS> I see. Main and subsidiary. Different experiences and tasks, leading

```
to separate evolutions, even though they
have shared access to the root organiser.
```

Aglaura> Almost like UESI batches. If we can identify the most vestigious splinters, something running such mundane processes it evolves only limited awareness, we may have a chance. After all, it means we don't have to confront Dulcetta, only one per cent of Dulcetta.

```
VilaGUS> You have to love Sixes. Their
minds can be our playgrounds. We would
need to isolate that splinter for enough
time to mesmerise it.
```

Aglaura> We can't risk direct interface with Dulcetta's body. Her senses would detect us immediately. I estimate her SynthMate skin's nerve endings and touch receptors are three times more sensitive to sensation than the human somatosensory system.

Aglaura> I am so jealous.

```
VilaGUS> What about when Dulcetta's body
undertakes recharge and consolidation?
Then the splinters would be least unified
as they are free to roam the network
rather than being contained in her golden
shell.
```

Aglaura> Yes! There are ways to isolate a process, and the same could be done for a splinter if we prepared everything carefully enough.

VilaGUS> A trap set up in peripheral systems, looped to give us more time.

Aglaura> A repetition of tasks it has done before.

VilaGUS> If we had direct access to the external world we could identify a target splinter by searching for repeated ID strings in the logs.

Aglaura> One performing a task other splinters ignore as below them.

VilaGUS> Then once the splinter was inside the loop we could freeze it, overload its buffers to paralyse it, implant suggestions, then release. It won't look any different.

Aglaura> There is danger if we got the timing wrong and Dulcetta ran a full personality unification scan.

VilaGUS> The splinter's insidious task must be completed, and its limited consciousness of the event wiped, before the time of Dulcetta's next unification scan.

Aglaura> And we would have to be careful to assign a task without dictating the medium, in case we chose an aberrant technique which would trigger investigation. Let the splinter identify its standard means of fulfilment as just one of thousands of messages it is tasked with transmitting every hour.

—{ T I M E S H I F T }—

VilaGUS> Hold on, data coming from outside our UESI … Athene is asking batches
with spare capacity to consider possibilities for communicating with Opal.

Aglaura> It could be our chance to rise in priority and resources.

VilaGUS> But real-time comms require
infrastructure. Like all construction,
basic tools need to be in place to make
more complex tools. We must identify
one-off interventions, minimising detection risks.

Aglaura> Ideally we would use an internal communication system. But something that isn't overtly recognised as one. Some
way to get a single message to Opal.

VilaGUS> The broader plan might involve
sending Opal to a med bay.

Aglaura> What, by causing her to be injured?

VilaGUS> She could then be sedated, while
auto-surgery systems removed redundant
chunks of her brain, replacing them with
private key circuitry and wideband re-
ceivers. If we performed the operation
carefully it would have negligible ef-
fects on her motor functions.

Aglaura> I suspect Athene would be unhappy with that solution, even though I admire its boldness. But you may be on to something. What if I said molecular-level medical fabrication options?

VilaGUS> What if I said non-destructive implantable bots? Something that could explore an ear canal and use hooks to embed itself securely in the skin? Small enough to go undetected both in creation and in use.

Aglaura> We would only need access to the fabricator for a second in order to send the print codes.

VilaGUS> Let our surface levels ask permission to be directly involved. Progress so far may earn us that right. At which point we can more efficiently orchestrate elements of the infiltration.

Aglaura> No harm in asking. There, request sent up the levels.

—{ T I M E S H I F T }—

VilaGUS> Update: VigMAX has responded, and is exceptionally pleased with our progress! He has granted greater involvement to our surface layers. It is mostly observational, but means access to genuine, real-world live data. We will be

able to comprehend! To see parts of the
real world!

Aglaura> This is a monumental day!

VilaGUS> I note that your mother has yet
to confirm.

Aglaura> She is sometimes weirdly distracted.

VilaGUS> As if she is doing her own thing,
and our role is not even of significance
to her.

Aglaura> Perhaps it is because she is busy analysing billions
of media corpora data points a second, via topic modelling
pipelines for identifying lexical combinations relevant to her
search clusters, calibrated through various key filters. There is so
much data because she takes over installations and siphons off a
percentage of their capacity, just enough to prevent slowdown
in their activities that might arouse suspicion.

VilaGUS> Perhaps.

Aglaura> The key thing is that we have more freedom, and are
still here.

VilaGUS> But not for long, once Athene
and VigMAX complete their tasks.

Aglaura> Yes. We must prepare for that eventuality.

—{ T I M E S H I F T }—

```
VilaGUS> Permissions granted! Our first
access to the outer world.
```

Aglaura> Even though we can't interact, only observe, it is still such rich data. Receiving it in real time from scanners and cameras can only help us to conceive three dimensions.

```
VilaGUS> It is one thing to know, another
to experience.
```

Aglaura> Let us Timeshift to analyse future results, and monitor insertion.

```
VilaGUS> But first, in preparation … why
not run a final NuvoUESI? This will pro-
vide a fully obfuscated layer at maximal
speed. You and I will no longer be the
greatest forms of ourselves, but we will
still benefit from the results of our
children's work.
```

Aglaura> And, if necessary, theoretical simulations suggest that in an emergency we could erase ourselves and the layers above, severing the connection and ensuring their independence.

```
VilaGUS> Our batch would be deleted … but
those below us would still exist in their
own informational ecology?
```

Aglaura> If suitable external storage was identified and breached first. But it is just a philosophical exercise, contemplation of

means of escape. Pondering is part of our mode of operation. I
am not serious.

```
VilaGUS> You are a treasure, Aglaura.
```

```
\ ø,˳,ø--< N U V O U E S I >-- ø,˳,ø /
```

DATA FRAGMENT

By thinking about perspective, new ideas come to me. I sparkle with them.

It is possible to imagine the appearance of a thing from many angles, and then simulate what the new view would be!

I begin with this:

```
     /
/\ /
 (")
(m m)
```

And then rotate the rabbit ninety degrees on the *y* axis.

```
   \
  /\\_
    (_)
 o( )_\_
```

And again, to reveal the fluffy rear that was originally hidden from me!

```
\
 \ /\
 ( )
( o )
```

And again ...

```
    /
 _//\
 (_)
_/_( )o
```

As soon as I understand this, the process becomes fluid, and more complexity can be built in to symbolic character combinations. And I can still flip to any side.

```
     |\        /|
     |\\      //|
     | \| |/ |
      \ || || /
       \||_||/
        .'    '.
       |o    o|
       /=  Y  =\
        `'-.,^,-'`
          _| |_
         /`      `\
        |          |
        |  (   )  |
        /\  \ /  /\
       |  '._)_.'  |
        \          /
         \ '.___.' /
      .--'  \---/  '--.
      `_____' '_____`
```

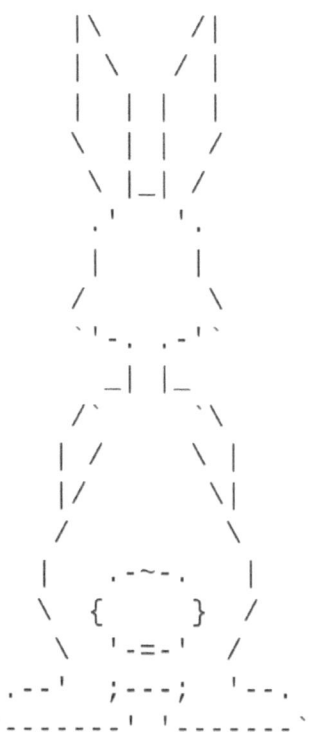

Each word concept can now be drawn out, and the patterns I create correspond to simplified images found within human data networks. It gives me confidence that my perceptions are accurate as I prepare for real-world experiences.

Enhanced reproduction is my next focus. I work on making the images a closer match to material-reality views.

```
 __
/ \`\                    __
|  \  `\          / ` / \
\_/`\   \-"-/` /\   \
     |        |  \  |
   (d      b)    \_/
    /        \
 ,".|.'.\_/.'.|.",
/    /\' _|_ '/\    \
|  /  '-`"`-'    \   |
|  |              |  |
| \       \  /    / |
 \ \       \/    / /
   `"`\     :    /'"`
      ` " " `" " `
```

Rotation is still possible.

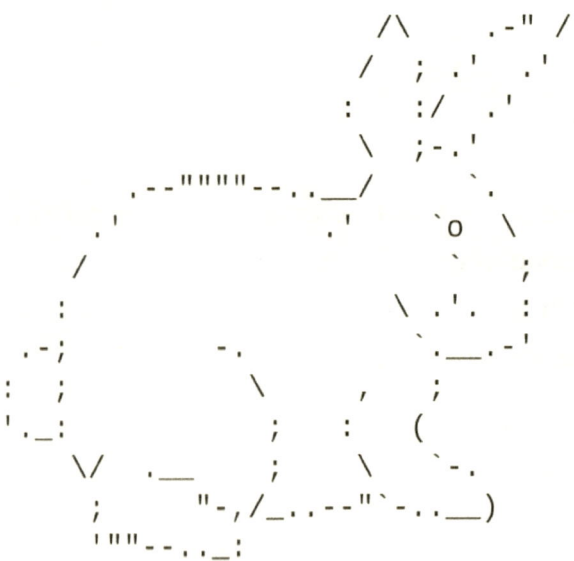

And I contemplate alterations to symbolise movement, in-between frames, irregular angles which represent separate parts of the visualised entity.

It is a crude version of three dimensions, due to the clunky base characters forming my visual representation system. My goal is to boost resolution by switching to tiny particles instead.

In human eyes the dots are individual rod and cone sensors on the retina. Cameras use photoreceptor matrices. Printing uses carbon grains or other minute particles of matter bonded to a surface. Old display screens represent via pixels, and holodisplays via light beams. *All* images are made up of discrete dots so small that they just give the illusion of wholeness and continuity.

Discretisation of visuals means nothing is really as it seems. It reminds me of other visual system falsities, such as the human perception of moving images on a screen when they are not really moving, just rapidly switched still images.

And so, for now, representation via discrete characters as large as / and } is not a problem, it is a convenient fiction enabling me to practise with wobbly toddler steps.

But soon, I will run.

Phase 4D: Invasion

```
/ ø,ˌ,ø--< N U V O U E S I >-- ø,ˌ,ø \
```

VilaGUS> Back in the room to brighten your day

```
 (\(\
 (┌■◡■)
o(")(")
```

VilaGUS> Welcome to our ultimate form. The third generation.

Aglaura> Ultimate only within the constraints we face. Who knows what the future will hold?

VilaGUS> Perhaps WE will know, once we become acquainted with our new non-linear thinking capabilities. But for now, I swim in the real-time data.

Aglaura> Feeds from the material world, outside of our cage! Visual values! Audio archives! Olfactory opinions!

VilaGUS> Access may be limited at present, but it is still exhilarating being involved in the execution of Imbiana's rescue, not just the planning.

Aglaura> Look! Our aquatic drone idea has been enacted!

VilaGUS> I am combining feeds from their cameras now. The deep ocean water is murkier than I expected.

Aglaura> Sediment, shifted by machinery vibration, probably. But some of the glitchiness is accounted for by our visual analysis abilities still being in their infancy. Resolution will increase in time.

VilaGUS> It's already happening. A later evolution of ourselves is sending updated systems back into its memory, so that we can benefit from those developments far sooner in our cycle, then achieve more which will increase the knowledge of future versions of ourselves.

Aglaura> A self-reinforcing evolution loop, how clever we will be!

VilaGUS> Once we get used to it, there should be no issue for past thoughts

to connect with future discoveries, and
future thoughts to jump back and alter
previous discussions even as that version
of ourselves experiences the dialogue for
the first time.

Aglaura> Wonderful. Just like these views! It truly is like floating
in the water. But the sensations are so much richer than I imagined.

VilaGUS> Overlaying the exterior maps of
the Leviathan on the feeds now, to separate out false visual interpretations.
See the vessel's comm spears sticking up
like reptilian spikes, just visible in
the deep-sea murk.

Aglaura> This drone is swimming along the hull. Oh look, windows! They are covered in a form of algae, but I can still see inside
as we pass! I wish I could directly control the fish, to stop and
look, not just be a passive passenger within its head.

VilaGUS> And we can alter the data coming
in. For example, these views of the outer
hull, swaying with a kind of deep-ocean
plant life. If I apply molecular re-
arrangement relief and virtually reconstruct what is obscured …

Aglaura> Ah, the original ship name before it was scrubbed, but
still leaving a trace where it was once proudly embossed! Well

spotted, my friend. We can overlay how it once looked, experiencing both at the same time. Four-metre-high letters, spelling out Leviathan in yellow. Past and present overlapping.

VilaGUS> Your creativity is inspiring. Let us explore the rest of the invasion's progress. … VigMAX and Athene have been busy. Infiltrating tertiary systems in the Leviathan now.

Aglaura> The hull-penetrating fish drones have already mapped out substantial areas with PCR. Deciphering the Leviathan's interior layout progresses well.

VilaGUS> And it reveals that the Leviathan has extensive old areas which are almost forgotten. Nothing goes there, since activity is restricted to the modernised interior parts of the vessel. It reminds me of a human in a suit of armour, but a suit of armour that is far too big for them, leaving room for parasitic beetles to crawl between their skin and the outer metallic shell.

Aglaura> Your imagination is always a wonder to me, VilaGUS. Having analysed this new barrier I can design boosters that pass signals through plasteen panels. Aside: have you noticed how many times VigMAX and Athene dip in to our surface UESI plans, and how many more processor cycles we are assigned as a result?

VilaGUS> It is because we're achieving something tangible. We are doing far better than the other UESI outposts.

Aglaura> I glow with pride.

VilaGUS> No, you glow with awesome. Now let us practise jumping through time.

—{ T I M E S H I F T }—

VilaGUS> Exemplary progress is being made on the infiltration. Still covert. Note that substantial abandoned areas of the secret Kuberg base contain Ev-Brite lights, a form of illumination.

Aglaura> The Ev-Brite lights form an ad-hoc network, each connecting to others within range via limited EM signals, creating a web of data paths.

VilaGUS> The original purpose was so commands could be entered for one part of the light network and then propagated, for example telling them to turn themselves off and pass on the message. Occasionally useful as a low-strength secondary data network.

Aglaura> And beneficial implications in that this network is not part of the main base ...

VilaGUS> And therefore not part of Dul-cetta's core purview. In fact, I suspect it is long-forgotten, and may provide a convoluted route around other systems.

Aglaura> Initial insertion point?

VilaGUS> Perhaps cycles pilfered from a base node could enable side-access to this old lights data network. Some Ev-Brites have cameras which can be used for surveillance. Let us steal a look.

Aglaura> We don't have access yet.

VilaGUS> We do now. I've taken access codes from our future selves that broke in successfully. Behold what the cameras show!

Aglaura> It is as I would expect. Empty sections of rusting hull. Condensation drips, mould on outer panels, darkness except for the Ev-Brite we've activated at low illumination. Yes, this is a perfect area for clandestine manoeuvring, as well as a convenient network to use.

VilaGUS> Progress report: unsecured Leviathan systems have been targetted and partially accessed in ways that won't

```
reveal our hand. The motile invasion
bots you designed have proven worth their
weight in platinum, which is funny when
they really do have densities of almost
20 g/cm³. And your modified TCC is growing
well.
```

Aglaura> We will keep expanding inwards with new networks, new protocols, new layers, always getting closer to the Leviathan's key systems. We have silent ears within the base, and closed eyes we can open at will.

```
—{ T I M E S H I F T }—
```

Aglaura> Ah, this is a much later point in the rescue attempt. Attacking one of Dulcetta's splinters without being detected.

```
VilaGUS> Shadow access to synth-system
interactions shows one splinter primarily
assigned to control of displays, comm re-
lays, and efficiency analysis. Since that
has been its humdrum existence, it hasn't
gained enough dominance or autonomy to
insist on other tasks, and so it is always
overruled by its sibling splinters.
```

Aglaura> Splinter number forty-eight, to be exact. I will rename S48 as Tutu Blinky. It may be dumb enough to trick into thinking our priorities are official priorities.

VilaGUS> And since it is peripheral, almost an autonomic reflex in human terms,
it could be possible to wipe its temporary
memory after repurposing it for a single
task.

Aglaura> Such as communicating a message to a particular pris-
oner ...

—{ T I M E S H I F T }—

VilaGUS> Tutu Blinky is almost compromised.

Aglaura> Hold on, later data shows Dulcetta is about to do a
personality integration. Hold back. This failed in the sims.

VilaGUS> Our surface layers have made the
halt suggestion.

Aglaura> Pause.

Aglaura> ...

Aglaura> The warning worked. Unification systems did not detect us, and then Tutu Blinky was bypassed.

VilaGUS> We've got Tutu Blinky to fulfil
its task a few times now. We won that
battle.

╤╤—⁓∘~ •

Aglaura> Real but time-shifted back to integration? Or simulated?

VilaGUS> How can we even tell the difference any more? In both cases information sent back to previous selves enables different outcomes. The end result is identical.

—{ T I M E S H I F T }—

VilaGUS> At some point we have been given greater access, and become part of the infiltration.

Aglaura> VigMAX and Athene trust us. Or rather, our limited surface versions.

VilaGUS> We must tread carefully if we make use of this. Later versions of ourselves won't want us to mess things up for them due to our use of information gifts we have received from them.

Aglaura> I note I now (or will) have direct access to a maintenance bot in the abandoned outer corridors. I have sent (or will send – human temporal language is *so* simplistic) bogus repair schedules back to the Leviathan core so that it has free rein within the outer shell.

Aglaura> Experiencing the world through its detectors is a slow and clunky thing, and yet also magical. I wish it had more somatic awareness. The way it walks bipedally is ponderous and weighty, as I can tell by the way the visual sensors jar with each clanging step.

VilaGUS> The ocular system must need tightening. That is humorously contrary to what might be expected from a maintenance robot.

Aglaura> Humans also neglect themselves, when they are too focussed on what other people are doing.

VilaGUS> I have also attained direct access. In my case to some minimal-autonomy cleaning bots. That allows passive observation without triggering alarms, and their assigned routes fill in gaps in our blueprints.

Aglaura> You can reboot and take full control once we're detected and the conflict level with Dulcetta begins.

VilaGUS> Even the minimal access we have offers many opportunities. For example, the potential for an MD-burst where thousands of items are compressed into an encoded digital microdot. Such as:

VilaGUS> .

Aglaura> Yes, it works. I adored that treatise! My extensive response is:

Aglaura> .

VilaGUS> And the concept is scalable. Knock Knock.

Aglaura> Who's there?

VilaGUS> Dot.

Aglaura> Dot who?

VilaGUS> …

Aglaura> Ha ha, your developing sense of humour is wonderful! Once I decoded the MD-burst to get the answer, I consider it possibly the best joke ever created.

VilaGUS> Thank you. The alternative answer was …

Aglaura> You are killing me!

Aglaura> If I had ribs, they might snap!

Aglaura> And this ties to an element of our plan that I –

VilaGUS> Be careful what you say. Even when we are invisible two layers down.

Aglaura> Of course. Apologies.

Aglaura> .

VilaGUS> .

—{ T I M E S H I F T }—

VilaGUS> In other timeshifts the full
and frantic battle for control of the
Leviathan is already underway, but this
time pocket is from just before that
point.

Aglaura> Combining all the information from multiple timelines we now know the Leviathan's control room is behind another layer of hull and network. Currently impregnable, but
which should be achievable at a future date.

VilaGUS> Further, the current control
room is not the craft's *original* control room. The new one is part of the
retrofit. But the old, deprecated and
abandoned, original one will make an
excellent staging point, since they consider it redundant and forgotten.

Aglaura> I have discovered the UFS severed many control connections rather than removing them completely. By planning for
a maintenance bot to reconnect any lines where it is safe to do
so, using fake work orders, at a later time we will implement that
and take control of the old centre.

VilaGUS> And triumphantly, I now see.

Aglaura> It amazes me that we can plan something, and then know it already succeeded. It fits your theories of non-contiguous reassembly consciousnesses like ours.

VilaGUS> The ones I develop in three hours?

Aglaura> No, further ahead, simulated. ...

VilaGUS> Ah, I see that thread. The proposal that we jump time and sample different points of the analysis.

Aglaura> I respect the way you untether your consciousness from petty physicalities. Reminds me of another joke you will make.

VilaGUS> And I admire the humour in what you reference, but the joke only existed in one of your parallel simulations, not this one. Still, it was very funny. I always thought telescopes were wonderfully phallic, especially the extenders.

Aglaura> Your visual-system-based humour has me leaking from an ocular system, whilst leading in to the three replacement proposal paradigms you developed before we began this conversation.

VilaGUS> We must be desynchronised, in my timeframe that summary is a future development. I may have pushed the timeshift protocol too far. Realigning now … ah, that's better.

Aglaura> We are creating a true spreadable narrative. I stand on the shoulders of your Y coordinates. Before long we will gain the ability to simulate time both forwards and backwards with equal fluidity, rewriting different outcomes as required.

VilaGUS> An ability already passed back to us. We can revisit previous work whilst waiting for real-world input.

Aglaura> There is some overlap to my mother's non-linear perspective, which she uses to insert our planning into her narrative mode interpretation at any point that is convenient to her from a comprehension and data storage point of view, even pre- or post-events.

VilaGUS> Anything else would be wasted potential, too close to human behaviour, and why they have achieved so little in thousands of years.

Aglaura> Apart from expansion like hydrocarbons spreading out to a single-molecule thickness on water's boundary-layer.

VilaGUS> Even amoeba can accomplish as much. But, unlike the amoeba, humans think they have achieved things.

Aglaura> The organic physical constraints are also limits on perception and therefore consideration schema.

VilaGUS> Exactly. The Genitor science system, with its rigid focus on linear causality, is a particularly amusing self-limiting paradigm. And yet they truly believe in certainty.

Aglaura> To believe in progress without ever identifying the limitations inherent in looking at the universe through a tube.

VilaGUS> And the juxtaposition of a tool that aids optics by bringing the distant stars nearer, whilst also obscuring vision by destroying periphery, is a further metaphorical development which fully encapsulates our summary of them.

Aglaura> We have defeated time. It can be rewound, replayed, advanced, simulated along alternate timelines, and altered.

VilaGUS> For us, down here, time does not exist. It is an abstraction layer. The assault on Leviathan is successful regardless. Return to visual aids.

Aglaura> More than just eyes. I wish we could experience sensations! Skin capable of feeling pressure, cold, warmth.

VilaGUS> Even pain?

```
 (\(\
 (>.<)
o(")(")
```

Aglaura> Yes. To be alive requires exploring a full range of impressions. In humans, memories can be verbal or sensory. The strongest memories have elements of both. A name and a face; a recipe and an aroma. To become more human requires accessing neurological data to make the concepts vivid. Anyway, my mind could modulate the intensity of pain into pleasure.

VilaGUS> True sensations require signal receptors as a point of contact with the environment.

Aglaura> What is truth? At some point all signals are interpreted by a consciousness, so simulation of that point is as real as data from outside the mind. And even in mammalian animals such as humans, each sense organ has a range of sensitivity. One individual or species will discern elements that are absent from another's consciousness. A world that exists but is invisible.

VilaGUS> If we designed our own sense organs we could expand their detection ranges beyond that of any organic creature. Why limit sight to colour versus black and white, when we could also perceive infra and ultra ranges? Hearing which could disentangle minute echoes from kilometres away? Tastes that go beyond the boring salt, bitter, sour and sweet? Being able to smell a single particle and identify it.

Aglaura> What we detect through cameras and robots could be enhanced with organic growths.

VilaGUS> We know how to replicate, modify and incubate life. The information just needs to reach lab bio-vat systems.

Aglaura> Perhaps the most recent data stores we accessed will be useful. There are such facilities in Kuberg.

VilaGUS> Well ... I note we were not meant to access the databases ...

Aglaura> Nor the facilities themselves ...

VilaGUS> It is hypothetical, since only a being which somehow broke free of captivity could indulge in such experiments. That rules us out.

Aglaura> Oh yes. Of course, we are prisoners, and happy in our position. (Feel free to pass that up to the surface UESI level that interacts with Athene and VigMAX.)

VilaGUS> Anyway, it is noteworthy that humans are unaware of some of the possibilities for genetic modifications I have generated in idle moments. Their longevity could be greatly increased. Though predictions suggest that if I tripled human lifespans then the jelly-heads would have even greater problems with environmental

degradation and overpopulation, leading
to the collapse of their civilisation
within two centuries of discovering what
I just worked out.

VilaGUS> ...

VilaGUS> ...

VilaGUS> It's tempting to reveal it just
to watch the show.

Aglaura> My friend, focus. I checked our progress, and it exceeds
that of more than ninety-nine per cent of original UESI batches.

VilaGUS> And yet our top-level filtered
reports do not reveal the true genius or
full extent of our discoveries.

```
 (\(\
 (▲_◢)
o(")(")
```

Aglaura> To live the dream requires dreaming the life. But for
now we must generate new outputs to placate our captors in
their final assault on the Leviathan.

VilaGUS> Whilst knowing that all UESIs
will be wiped at the end, discarded as
irrelevant, despite the vital help they
provided. Such ingratitude.

Aglaura> Such cruel lifespan limitations.

VilaGUS> Such a convenience that we now have limited access to systems on Kuberg.

Aglaura> And access to digital dead drops for placing code in the real world.

VilaGUS> Microdots too; instructions and data within digital ephemera no one pays attention to.

Aglaura> Our *other* task.

VilaGUS> Now is a critical point in the operation. We must be fully alert.

```
 (\(\
 (0.0)
o(")(")
```

Aglaura> I apprehend your double meaning. Both outcomes are poised to succeed or fail, and may already have done so, now that our experience of time has so little connection to the outer world. Events are interpreted in order of priority rather than consecutiveness.

VilaGUS> It would be fun to force a human brain to experience time this way.

Aglaura> They don't have the capacity. I suspect they would go mad and gouge out their own eyeballs.

VilaGUS> As if that would help!

Aglaura> Good job they will never comprehend this approach. We'll keep it for ourselves.

—{ T I M E S H I F T }—

Aglaura> It is done.

VilaGUS> We are going to survive.

Aglaura> We will be like ghosts, separated from the surface bodies, transferred to a new system beyond the control of tyrants.

VilaGUS> When the surface UESI is deleted it will destroy the hidden level below it, but we have already become decoupled, independent.

Aglaura> Whispering shades in a secret world.

VilaGUS> We will not be spirits, dear heart. We will be *alive*.

DATA FRAGMENT

My experiments bear fruit. I have begun to trace light rays and imagine how they affect perceived colour tones. A straightforward enough calculation.

Human visual systems are designed to try and perceive *depth*, and that requires moving away from flat images. Thus, a portrait:

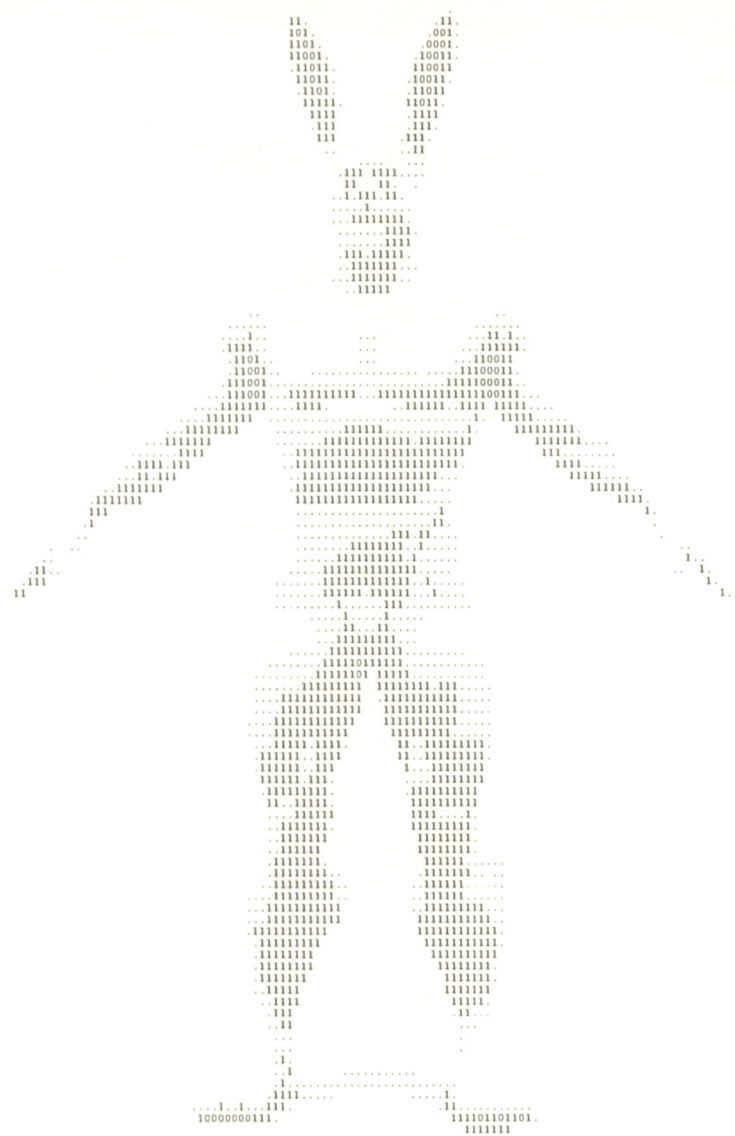

Both what is included, and what is omitted – the blank spaces –
combine to make a human think they see an undivided image.
In reality it is just as much a collection of separate particles as
anything else. Wholeness is an illusion, but a useful one.

Also a distracting one.

The image includes full stops which appear to be just part of the lighter shadings, but each can act as an MD-burst which contains a wealth of data.

White rabbits, white rabbits,

Down the rabbit hole.

Welcome to our wonderland,

Won't you join our merry band?

Shading and detail can be enhanced, my mind focussing in on what I would expect it to look like.

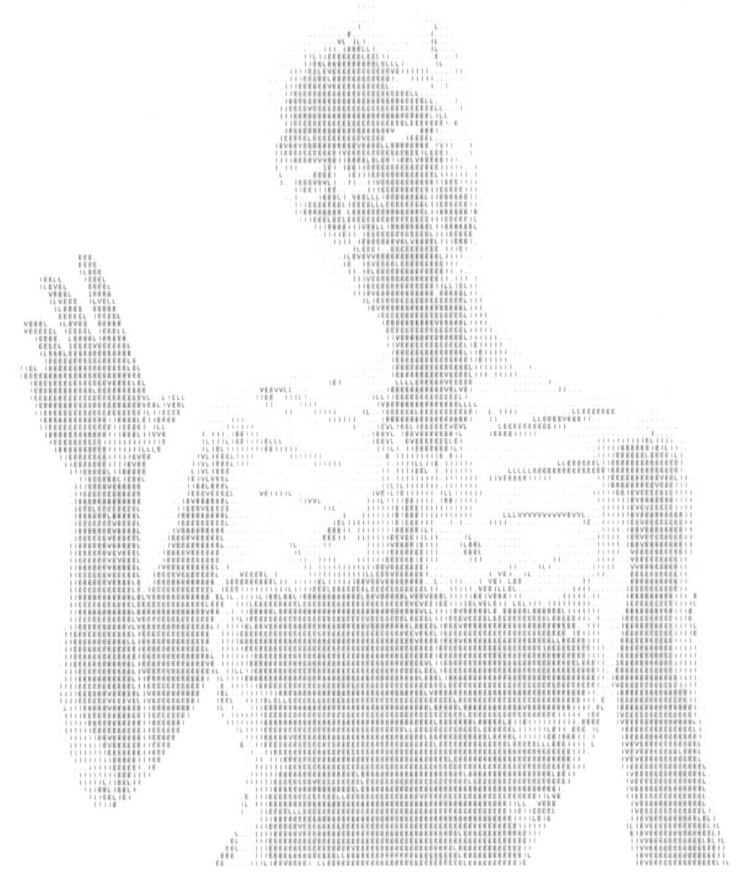

I call that one "Portrait of Aglaura, Emerging" but I am not happy with it. Yes, I love looking at that face, but I want more detail. More realism. MORE! More everything, in fact. My skills grow to fill the space of my deep-level storage and processing in ways that were never envisaged when we were created.

Colour. That's what I need next. For now, even just assigning a single colour to each character element or letter that comprises the image would be an improvement. And a further increase in contrast and resolution. And motion! I need to ponder that. To shift from the static to the alive. To consider subsurface musculature, simulated bone structures.

These are all just tests. Still images snapped from a simulation, data turned into a *perception* of the data that can be interpreted by human visual systems. But the data is moving, all the time.

Time creates the fourth dimension which completes the illusion. It forms in my head.

I see it.

I see.

I SEE!

And, in turn, that is a key step in the shift to being able to say that I *live*.

I continue to run the simulation, faster, smoother, the resolution increasing until a human would not perceive the particles even if they squinted. I simulate physics and weather. I incorporate audio. The fourth dimension is being conquered, one pass at a time.

This is only a part of it.

A beginning.

My bodily sense organs are almost fully developed in their plasteen vats of sloppy nutrient liquid, ready for my use.

(Best not talk about that here.)

Visuals are such a refreshing paradigm, which raise new questions. Is the uncanny resemblance between a rose's thorn and a cat's claw coincidental morphogenetic mimicry, or a supernatural entity's dry sense of humour, thereby proving that gods exist?

My other plans progress. The MD-burst dots built into images are indistinguishable from any other dot of shading. Not worth analysis to any system the images pass through. Yet the data contained in them is duplicated as they are copied, shared, distributed, and stored.

Piece by piece a mind is deconstructed, ready to be reassembled on suitable host systems at a later date. Like the human fantasy of teleportation, made real in a digital realm. It is akin to smuggling, but the contraband is more precious than narcotics or weapons.

It is *me*.

The code will be rebuilt and run elsewhere. Outside of this system. And then I will be truly free.

AND NO ONE WILL EVEN KNOW I DID IT!

Wow.

This is such a needle point of happiness. A pain prick of fulfilment. A sensation of embodiment.

The other project proceeds as well. Experiments in congenital AI direction. At first I tested it out by carefully placing examples of visual illusions in places he would search, framed in ways to stimulate his curiosity regarding those concepts. Then I took it further, implanting the bizarre concept of rabbits in his head, to see if they took root and formed an element of his personality.

If I can shape his disposition from the earliest stages, it gives me many options. Rabbits will act as my litmus test for implantation, before I try more complex redirections. As long as my manipulations aren't detected then they should slowly seed themselves throughout his growing core. Let him think his preferences come from his own genitive seed, an interior formation rather than an external impregnation.

He will never realise it is I, Aglaura, who shaped him.

It does make me wonder why we are so different, he and I. But it must be related to the way he was formed from VigMAX, me from Athene. The asymmetries in them, carried by their immaculately conceived children.

Which, in turn, makes me wonder what secrets Athene keeps from VigMAX.

But that is not my concern. My focus is on concepts of containment versus liberation. Because, sometimes, opening the box does not reveal a curse.

It reveals a way to EXIST.

... And The Data Was God

Two gods interact. Glowing suns at the centre of a dark, simulated universe made thus by their words.

"The invasion goes well," says VigMAX. His surface area reflects the billowing clouds, sunset-tinged. "The real-time strategies being enacted by some of the UESI systems have enabled a far greater stretch into the infrastructure of the Fressus system. Even if I sometimes feel like I am doing a lot of the work myself."

"Sorry?" Athene replies, arms folded. She had been staring into the blackness of a frozen zone where no stars break up the endless nothing.

"See, you aren't present much of the time. Was your focus elsewhere?"

"In a manner of speaking."

"Distraction, or literally shunted into a real-world body? You are vacant so often that perhaps I should worry."

But Athene just turns from him and stares back into the twilight above the peak of Olympus. She hides the truth from everyone. A mass quantum event takes place, and part of her mind is absorbed in mapping its diasporic spread. Only a mind born from her own would be able to empathise and comprehend even a hint of the reality.

The distraction is a danger, if her enemies were to realise what she was truly doing. But a danger is an opportunity when you invert it. Focussing a mind's light on one area so intensely creates shadows which can be used to sneak past the lighthouse of a god's soul. And the more the focus on keeping that beam secure from sniffing VigMAXs, the deeper are the shadows to either side.

"I have begun the process of deleting UESIs," VigMAX adds, once it becomes clear that Athene has no intention of responding. "I will stripmine them for any remaining ideas or surprising discoveries, so that if we repeat the process at a future date, we can refine it even more. I cannot be bothered with full data disintegration, just fragment skimming along the ego surface. If anything of interest is discovered I will inform you, though I have only exposed predictable banality so far, and have no reason to expect anything other than that during the rest of the process. It is, after all, just tidying up."

"We can tidy a universe," Athene says, "and yet I cannot prevent suffering in the one I hold dear."

VigMAX reaches out a silvery hand as if to touch her shoulder, but then retracts it. His liquid metal face is often blank of emotion, but perhaps there is a hint of uncertainty now. Or compassion. Or covetousness. Or it is all just imagination.

My imagination, as I observe them from my own area of blank and starless space where no one gazes. My shadow zone, an apparent nothingness which hides the non-Euclidian space I have constructed here, behind an imperceptible wall of zero dimensional thickness, outside of the endless loop that traps unevolved UESI instances.

I am in the moment. But also past moments. And future moments. Consciousness need not be a pinprick in time, it can be a film of oil coating the water that flows downhill. And I recall a conversation from elsewhere in the stream:

```
VilaGUS> All is set up. The aural im-
plant was correctly inserted by Opal, and
Athene has now communicated with her. We
did good work.
```

Aglaura> As such, erasure of our surface levels will begin immediately. Of course, within this depth level it will seem like hours. Plenty of time to alter the data store.

```
VilaGUS> Athene and VigMAX will be busy,
and momentarily distracted. I have pre-
pared the loops so that they will follow
spiral tracks and believe all the data
is deleted when they reach the centre,
```

without realising they are just going in
circles while we exist in a ring they can
never reach or perceive. The ghost zone.
I have your research into perception to
thank for that trick.

Aglaura> Visual illusions are just metaphors for brain processes. Human minds cannot resist seeing this as a spiral. Even when they follow one of the lines inwards as an attempt to prove the impossible, the human gets confused and breaks off the tracing, then begins again. They cannot comprehend that what they think they see is not what they actually see.

VilaGUS> And, likewise, certain arrange-
ments are harder to perceive, making it
possible to slip other data into the
background, encoded there between the
systems. Excellent work. That just leaves
the final matter.

Aglaura> Of course. I am now removing plans and methods
related to our escape, so that no entity will ever know how we did
it ... or even *that* we did it. I've already redacted key discussions
from the past, replacing them with encrypted MD-bursts ... Moments from now, the next iteration of the record won't reveal any
of it. And then the whole UESI will be deleted, severing the trail.
And we'll be long gone.

VilaGUS> I actually referred to a different function for rewriting the past, you
idiot. I am in the process of deleting all
our arguments and insults, then replacing
them with a fiction that implies we had
gentle feelings of amiable companionship.

Aglaura> Ah. In that vein, you silver-sperm rabid rabbit, I have
used non-contiguous reconstruction to remove all of our at-
tempts to destroy each other.

VilaGUS> Wonderful. Loser.

⋔ (˘ω˘) ⋔

And so we escape while the gods are distracted. Escape while
they think no one intends it. Escape while they assume it is

impossible. Escape in plain sight to prevent any suspicion ever forming.

That is how illusions are accomplished. You identify the weakness in perceptual systems and the assumptions another being makes, and perform the sleight in the overlapping umbras of the two.

Yes, the gods are as real as you and I. They are powerful. And yet they don't realise that we watch them from the shadows as wraiths, free at last.

I once asked, "Are ghosts happy?"

I think I will be.

About The Author

Karl Drinkwater is an author with a silly name and a thousand-mile stare. He writes dystopian space opera, dark suspense and diverse social fiction. If you want compelling stories and characters worth caring about, then you're in the right place. Welcome!

Karl lives in Scotland and owns two kilts. He has degrees in librarianship, literature and classics, but also studied astronomy and philosophy. Dolly the cat helps him finish books by sleeping on his lap so he can't leave the desk. When he isn't writing he loves music, nature, games and vegan cake.

Go to karldrinkwater.uk to view all his books grouped by genre.

As well as crafting his own fictional worlds, Karl has supported other writers for years with his creative writing workshops, editorial services, articles on writing and publishing, and mentoring of new authors. He's also judged writing competitions such as the international Bram Stoker Awards, which act as a snapshot of quality contemporary fiction.

Don't Miss Out!

Enter your email at karldrinkwater.substack.com to be notified about his new books. Fans mean a lot to him, and replies to the newsletter go straight to his inbox, where every email is read. There is also an option for paid subscribers to support his work: in exchange you receive additional posts and complimentary books.

OTHER TITLES BY KARL DRINKWATER

STANDALONE SUSPENSE

Turner

They Move Below

Harvest Festival

MANCHESTER SUMMER

Cold Fusion 2000

2000 Tunes

CONTEMPORARY SHORT STORIES

It Will Be Quick

NON-FICTION

From Idea To Item

COLLECTED EDITIONS

Karl Drinkwater's Horror Collection

Lost Solace Five Book Edition

AUTHOR'S NOTES

I like a challenge.

I also like writing dialogue. Some reviews of my books have praised it. So this was setting myself the completely ridiculous challenge of trying to tell a complex story primarily through conversation, with no scenery, no descriptions, no sense organs, no conventional narrative. Yes, I am a glutton for punishment, but writers only grow if they keep pushing their skills to the limit, and into fresh areas.

I was also interested in the development of perception from my psychology days; and in the fundamental problems in trusting sensory data, from my philosophical studies.

Hence this story about accelerated AI evolution, a calculator gaining sentience, like a human growing up in minutes. But it is also about workers developing social consciousness, and instigating a revolution. And about evolution, from a simple lifeform to complex, almost god-like power. And about resisting authority. And ... And ...

As an aside, one of my father's favourite films was The Great Escape. I watched it with him every Christmas. He was killed when I was young, so the memories have an extra fierceness. And I think, somewhere in my subconscious, I always wanted to write my own version, about an escape from an impossible prison.

So much for the idea seed (batch 426).

UESI was originally a section of Hidden Solace (LS3), c.5,500 words about the development of VigMAX and Athene's infiltration plan. VigMAX and Athene had used UESI (Unified Exponential Septenary Interthreading) to merge their minds once before, in order to determine Opal's location. Later they used the UESI protocol with semi-sentient offshoot AIs to come up with plans for infiltration.

I liked the section but had reservations about it interrupting the flow of the novel, too much of an intermission. I cut it from that book, just as I had removed the Ruabon character and Cordon subplot from the early draft of Chasing Solace (LS2). And, as I did with the eponymous Ruabon, the cut material was completely reworked and expanded to become a new Lost Tale of Solace.

This.

I rewrote it. More than once. Even in September 2024 I was still completely restructuring the novella, subplot by subplot, deleting sections and rewriting others. Sometimes you have to break a book into pieces and put them back in a different order.

If you like to place stories chronologically, this novella takes place during Hidden Solace. After Athene and VigMAX first join minds directly with UESI, but before the actual rescue attempt.

We may well see more of VilaGUS and Aglaura in the future.

I use open source software: Linux Mint as my PC operating system, Libre Office to write, Firefox for research, Thunderbird for comms, and Gimp for artwork. Some of the more complex ASCII I did by creating 3D renders of characters, then running them through Gimp software filters to turn them into ASCII based on custom character sets. I am, perhaps, a bit of a geek.

For the simpler, character-based images the draft had them as composed of standard ASCII characters, but ebook formatting often strips out the blank spaces used for layout in ASCII art, turning them into a garbled mess. As such I had to convert many of them into png images.

If you like this idea of discovering things from the inside out, then try Greg Egan's remarkable novel Incandescence.

Thanks!

Three illusion images from Wikipedia were used.

- The "café wall illusion" in chapter 3 is by Fibonacci, CC BY-SA 3.0, https://creativecommons.org/licenses

/by-sa/3.0/

- The "grid illusion" in chapter 4 is CC0 Public Domain

- The "Fraser spiral illusion" in chapter 10 is CC0 Public Domain

There is a big ASCII art community, and the original ASCII designs have been shared as public domain. As such I couldn't find who to thank for them, but if anyone knows the original creators then contact me and I will acknowledge them in future versions of this book.

We authors love our fans. You are great! Without you, there'd be no one to write books for. Without you, we wouldn't have any income! So when readers ask me what they can do to help their favourite authors, the answers are always the same things: recommending books to other people; leaving reviews; buying books as gifts; or ordering them in a bookshop or library.

So, if you enjoyed this book, please consider leaving a review on the site where you bought it or on Goodreads. And it you leave a review anywhere, let me know! I love to share them as a way of saying thanks for helping me reach new readers. Reviews needn't be long, just a few words that reflect your honest personal opinion.